The
Christmas
Bike

The Christmas Bike

Tara Mayoros

SWEETWATER
BOOKS

An Imprint of Cedar Fort, Inc.
Springville, Utah

ISBN 13: 978-1-4621-1932-5

Published by Sweetwater Books, an imprint of Cedar Fort, Inc.
2373 W. 700 S., Springville, UT 84663
Distributed by Cedar Fort, Inc., www.cedarfort.com

LIBRARY OF CONGRESS CATALOGING-IN-PUBLICATION DATA
Names: Mayoros, Tara, 1977- author.
Title: The Christmas bike / Tara Mayoros.
Description: Springville, Utah : Sweetwater Books, An imprint of Cedar Fort, Inc., [2016] | Includes bibliographical references and index.
Identifiers: LCCN 2016028923 (print) | LCCN 2016032875 (ebook) | ISBN 9781462119325 (perfect bound : alk. paper) | ISBN 9781462127108 (epub, pdf, mobi)
Subjects: LCSH: Gifts--Fiction. | Bicycles--Fiction. | Christmas stories. | LCGFT: Novels.
Classification: LCC PS3613.A965 C48 2016 (print) | LCC PS3613.A965 (ebook) | DDC 813/.6--dc23
LC record available at https://lccn.loc.gov/2016028923

Cover design by Michelle May Ledezma
Cover design © 2016 Cedar Fort, Inc.
Edited and typeset by Jessica Romrell

Printed in the United States of America

10 9 8 7 6 5 4 3 2 1

Printed on acid-free paper

To my sisters.

Our homemade Christmas gifts to each other are always my favorite.

Here's mine to you.

Chapter One

Bloom where you're planted. Bloom where you're planted. The mantra rang through my head as I walked through the door to see my husband and three young kids after another long day at work.

I longed to see the sun after days of waking up well before dawn and sweating in a sugar-filled kitchen at the bakery, missing the sandstone sun as it dripped below the dusty horizon before I could leave.

"Looks like tomorrow will be another beautiful Christmas Eve," the weatherman said over the TV in the family room. "Temperatures in the high eighties. Santa will be coming to Phoenix wearing flip flops and shorts."

How could I bloom in a place that scorched tender leaves and shriveled up shallow roots?

I leaned against the wall and watched as my kids draped over the couch with homework strewn all over the carpet. Our little Christmas tree in the corner stood without ornaments.

Yes, I'd become tender and shallow; I'd worked to the brittle bone to be able to help dig us out of our financial hole.

During the crazy month of December, my husband and I hadn't even had time to bring in the Christmas decorations that were stored in plastic boxes outside.

I rubbed my face with one hand that smelled like peppermint frosting. Balancing a bakery box in the other hand, I walked in to greet my family.

"Why didn't you come to my Christmas party at school today?" my middle son asked.

I tried to smother the monstrous guilt of being a working mother as I felt it spark in my veins. I placed the box of broken cookies and imperfect frosted cupcakes on the kitchen table. Hopefully they would be penance for my failures.

I sighed. *Sugar fixes everything.* It was the slogan for the bakery, after all. And I'd stared at the framed slogan poster in the shop for days, weeks, months. I'd seen customers, young and old, with their faces alight with the lure of tempting treats and sweet seduction that promised to fix everything.

I will *fill my house with love and laughter this Christmas.* Maybe cookies were the answer.

I lifted up half a chocolate chip cookie and gave it to him. "I'm so sorry but—"

"I know, I know. You had to work," he said grabbing the cookie. I wrapped him in my arms before he could get away and looked up at my other two kids who also had parties I had missed out on.

"Let's get those decorations out," I said with a smile that I didn't quite feel.

Brent stood from the couch and announced in a voice that made all the kids giggle. "I can help with that."

Hand in hand we walked to the side of the house and then pulled the faded tarp off of a few plastic bins. Brent grabbed two and I grabbed one.

"Marie," Brent said to me. "Do you smell that?" He stopped and placed the boxes on the dirt.

I sniffed and dropped mine. "What the—"

"Oh rats," Brent said, pointing.

"Huh?"

"No really. Look, there have been rats in here."

I looked inside the open Christmas bin and, sure enough, fuzzy mouse nests and little black spots covered everything.

"Oh no!" I lifted my box lid. Melted candles covered the garlands and the Christmas tree ornaments. Cross-stitched stockings from my mother and a homemade quilt were all drizzled with red and green wax. With heavy heart I looked at the other box where the plastic had become cracked and brittle, baked from the heat of Phoenix; it had been an open door for rats and other critters.

My shoulders sagged as I looked at my decade-old collection of Christmas décor that was now ruined.

"This might be the only salvageable thing," Brent said to me, holding up a tin box that I knew had a Christmas Nativity from Jerusalem inside. "It's been sealed, but you'll still want to sanitize it."

"We can't tell the kids," I whispered and thought fast. "I forgot to get a few stocking stuffers on my way home. I'll go grab them and a few Christmas tree ornaments at the grocery store. There are cheap ones there."

I didn't even know how to store Christmas décor without it getting ruined. Another example of why I couldn't bloom in the desert.

Chapter Two

Moments later I pulled into the parking lot of the grocery store a few miles from my house. My car rattled a bit before I switched off the key and went inside.

My favorite Christmas carol, "I Heard the Bells on Christmas Day," chimed over the store speakers.

I heard the bells on Christmas Day
Their old familiar carols play,
And wild and sweet the words repeat
Of peace on earth, good will to men.

A fifty-dollar bill burned inside my pocket. Could I get everything we needed for under fifty dollars? I grabbed a cart and walked down the aisles, humming along with the song while taking inventory for every last penny I'd spend.

I thought of the night before. *Who'd left that fifty-dollar bill, along with a Christmas plate of baklava, and doorbell ditched us?*

I stopped humming and thought hard. Only a few people knew of our financial situation. From the outside we probably seemed stable, and maybe we were, to a point. But no matter how long or hard Brent and I worked, it never seemed to be enough to make ends meet. Anything nice that we still had was left over from our years of plenty.

Whoever it was that gave us such a charitable contribution knew me well enough to know that baklava was my favorite dessert. *Who knew that about me?* As I walked down the aisles, I thought of names and came up short. That would remain a secret until I watched the video of my life in heaven. That is, if I made it to heaven; God knew I had so many imperfections and was a failure of a mother.

At the checkout line I eyeballed the price monitor. Every once in a while, to stay within the budget, I returned to the cashier a few things I didn't especially need.

"$50.01," the cashier said to me.

I sighed in relief and handed her the fifty-dollar bill, smiling proudly to myself at how good I'd become at frugality. I dug through my purse, looking for a stray penny. *There must be one in here somewhere . . .*

I felt a tap on my shoulder.

"Here," said a woman's voice. "You look like you could use this."

A woman stood in a silk tank top behind me in the line. Wrapped around her aged leather skin, I noticed her silver and turquoise jewelry. My favorite. Probably something she'd purchased from the neighboring Indian Reservation. I liked her right away. Her vivid blue eyes, tucked inside wrinkles and laugh lines, looked at me with concern. She placed something in my hands.

I glanced down and saw a coupon for ten dollars back when you spend fifty.

My emotions swelled in my chest and they threatened to flood from my eyes. I lowered my head and ruffled through my purse as if I was searching for something, which I was . . . *where's that blasted penny?* I blinked a few times to dam the tears.

"Thank you," I said quietly, staring at her matching bracelet to avoid her sky-blue gaze.

Who cries over a ten-dollar *coupon?* Apparently me.

How did she know I needed that? Did I have charity case written on my forehead? I had tried so hard to put on a mask of pride and independence. If strangers could see through it so quickly, what did my friends think? I'd need to work on that more.

I swiped at my cheek, which was hot from embarrassment, before looking up at the kind woman. I tried to brush it off that it wasn't a big deal by casually laughing as I handed the cashier the coupon. She handed me a crisp ten dollar bill back because I'd spent one penny over fifty dollars.

"Don't worry about the penny," she said to me with a wink.

"Thank you," I said to both the cashier and the woman behind me. "Every little bit helps, right?" I smiled with nonchalance.

I didn't think I fooled the older woman at all because she asked me if there was more she could help with. I pretended not to hear as I walked away with my bag toward the door.

I wasn't a charity case.

When I got to my car I turned the car key over and over in the ignition, but it didn't start. I gripped the steering wheel and even punched it.

Was I a charity case?

The kind woman with the amazing jewelry crossed behind my car. She paused when she saw me stranded. I cranked down my window because, yes, it didn't have power windows, and waved through the dark.

"Thanks again." I smiled.

That seemed to satisfy her and she disappeared behind other cars.

I stopped a couple of people to ask for a jump, but everyone seemed so hurried and said they didn't have jumper cables anyway.

At some point, the repair bills stacked up against this car wouldn't be worth it to fix anymore. Thankfully, my husband was an above average mechanic, as he'd proved himself to be time and time again. *What a guy. I really lucked out*, I thought as I called his number to have him come rescue me.

"Hi babe," he said.

I tried to talk, but couldn't.

"Marie? Are you okay?"

I nodded, although he couldn't see. "My car." I squeaked out.

He sighed. "I'll be right there."

Crossing my arms, I leaned against the hood of my car, waiting for the parking spot in front of me to clear so that I could reserve the spot for my husband. This wasn't our first go around of towing cars or jumping batteries.

I ran my hands through my brown hair, which was pulled up in a messy bun, and realized I had dried frosting on my upper arm. I scratched it off as I waited impatiently for Brent.

The car ahead backed away and I stood in the crowded parking spot until familiar headlights pulled in.

I plastered on a weary smile. I'd shown him too many tears over the years, especially since moving to Phoenix earlier this year, and I'd made it a point to not let him see me cry. I was proud that the ruined decorations hadn't gotten the best of me.

Some things were unbearable for him to watch. Like, for instance, me not being able to paint as much as I used to, or spend lazy days reading my favorite books, or making crafts with the kids. I was a full-time working mother now who worked overtime during the holidays. I'd show some grit.

He enveloped me in an embrace, sniffed at my hair, and pulled back. "Molasses cookies. Mmm, my favorite."

"There are a couple broken ones at home."

"Oh goodie," he said, smiling into my eyes. When he saw that I wasn't in the mood for sweet, sugary conversation, he walked back to the trunk of his car and pulled out jumper cables. "Pop the hood."

I did as he said and after a few attempts of jumping the battery, the car moaned back to life. Brent rolled up the jumper cables and then gave me a quick kiss on the lips. "You have the ornaments?"

I nodded.

"Okay, I'll see you at home."

"Thanks, hon."

He winked and then folded back into the driver's seat and pulled away.

As I drove home I took inventory of any missing items and realized that I'd checked off everything on my mental list. I'd become list happy but my organization of managing a bakery didn't quite seep into my personal life. Except for lists. I was a master of writing lists. Everywhere else I was a wreck, always missing my kid's practices, their book reports, or the bus stops.

But I didn't want to think about that now. Both Brent and I had the holiday off. I'd promised myself that I would make it blissful.

We could spend time with the kids, decorate the tree, go for walks, ride our bikes, and watch movies. Driving home, I smiled, thinking about the many things I had planned. Even though the kids wouldn't have much this year—or hardly any decorations out—I'd make it a point for them to have our home filled with love and laughter. We'd bake in the kitchen, deliver homemade treats to our neighbors, and fill the warm desert sky with Christmas carols.

Chapter Three

The next morning, my three kids gathered in the kitchen as I whipped up French toast. They were fighting one another for my attention to look at their Christmas projects from school.

"How about I hang all of them on the fridge," I finally said.

I went back to preparing the skillet and mixing the eggs.

"Can I help? Can I, can I?" Anthony, my youngest, asked. My two older kids had already decided artwork hanging on the fridge wasn't as cool for them as it used to be. My heart pinched as I watched them walk into the family room with longing. They were getting so tall. And neither one of them believed in Santa anymore.

"Sure, Anthony. Wash your hands and then pull up a chair."

Soon he was by my side dipping the bread into the eggs and making a complete mess. I cringed when I caught myself scolding him for not coating the bread perfectly. Everything was easier when I just did it myself. But then guilt weaved into my thoughts because I'd promised myself to fill this house with love and laughter this holiday. I let it go and focused on his excited eyes and the fact that we were spending time together.

"Great job," I said, smiling.

"Do you think I could work at the bakery?"

"I think you could do whatever you decide to do. If that's working in a bakery, then I'll help you get there." *Oh please no. Have greater aspirations, please.* I loved my job, I really did. It just didn't allow me to afford everything on my children's Christmas lists.

I walked to the fridge to take out a stick of butter to coat the skillet. There was none left so I grabbed a bit of oil instead and coated the pan. I'd have to go to the store after breakfast. I thought about my dead car that sat in the driveway.

"Hey," I said, leaning into Anthony, whispering to him like I had a great secret. "How about me and you bike to the grocery store after breakfast?"

His eyes lit up.

I pressed my fingers to my lips and winked. He glanced into the family room at the older kids and he nodded. Of all my kids, my baby in first grade suffered the most from me working so much. The older two could still remember a time when I didn't work. We had spent countless hours outside, or in the mountains, or hanging by a pool. But that was before Phoenix . . . when we had more time together . . . and when our Christmases were more extravagant.

"You excited to go ice blocking later today?" I asked him.

He nodded again with greater excitement, making his blond curls, still highlighted from the sun, bounce.

Ice blocking on the day of Christmas Eve was a tradition that my friends had started years before our move to Phoenix. We were new to it. None of us lived near family and so we became one another's family. We were excited to gather all of our kids, buy blocks of ice, and then head to a park with hills. I'm sure the thrills were going to be just as exciting as sledding on snow. I loved the friends I had made.

Remembering the potluck, I grabbed my phone and texted my friend that I'd bring the rolls to go along with her chili. Then I sent her a funny photo of a man dressed up as Santa riding a bike in a speedo.

Ice blocking and chili tailgate party with friends? What could be better?

I smiled. Yes, living in Phoenix wasn't as dismal as I thought. Still, I knew my siblings and parents would be getting together tonight, acting out the Nativity like they did every year. I felt my smile droop. My heart broke a little every time I thought of them; I missed them terribly. I was very close to my sisters and my mother. Phone calls and texts never satisfied the constant ache to be near them.

I looked down at my son who was still smiling. *Don't think about missing family.*

It was time to fill this home with love and laughter.

Chapter Four

I have a few bucks in my wallet, if you need it," Brent said. "We won't be long. All I need is butter. Then we can leave for ice blocking," I said, giving him a kiss on the cheek.

I fished inside Brent's wallet, pulled out a couple dollars, and walked into the garage with Anthony on my heels. I pulled his helmet on his blond head and then we kicked up our kickstands. My bike was built for the mountains. I always felt silly riding it around the flat sidewalks of Phoenix. It was a decade old and showed its wear because my sisters and I had often gone riding up in the mountains together, pumping our bikes to the limit. They'd have exchanged their bikes for skis by now and would be skiing together this winter . . .

I sighed and looked into Anthony's anxious face. His missing teeth in that lop-sided grin would make anyone smile.

"Ready?"

"Yup!"

I placed my flip flop on the pedal and pushed behind Anthony as we made our way along the sidewalk. We wove along the neighborhood streets, looking at the dry creek beds and gravel landscaping. Christmas lights were wrapped around the trunks of palm trees and weaved in and out of cactus prickles. It took a very brave soul to decorate the saguaro or prickly pear plants, and yet so many did. Another example that I wasn't made of tough enough stuff to bloom in the desert.

Even the Acacia, Ironwood, and Mesquite trees had thorns. And the lovely fuchsia Bougainvillea? I looked down at some scratches on my fleshy arms. Well, the Bougainvillea had won the battle the other day when I'd tried to give it a winter haircut.

Every single plant in the desert wanted to kill me.

At least the scorpions were usually kept at bay during the "colder" winter weather. We'd killed over fifty scorpions the previous summer as our initiation to moving to Phoenix.

"Anthony," I said, trying to think of happier things. "Isn't this weather beautiful?" I lifted my hands off the handlebars and raised them high in the air. I'd learned to balance while riding on my bike when I was about his age.

He lifted one hand off of his handlebars. "Look!" he said. "I can do that too." His feet spun round and round, racing me down the road as we laughed.

Bike riding on Christmas Eve. How awesome is that? My face broke into the largest smile I'd felt in a long time.

The air was sharp with the smell of perfect weather. My muscles stretched beneath my skin, yawning with happiness. Days without exercising or seeing the sun had worn on my body. And to be perfectly honest, working at a bakery had made my body soft. But moments like riding bikes made me forget all my cares and focus on the now. I punched the air a few times and yelled out some of the excitement that made my heart beat faster. My son watched me and did the same. We both laughed when a neighbor, raking his rocks, looked at us with a strange set to his mouth.

When we reached the grocery store, I leaned Anthony's bike against the brick and placed mine on top. I couldn't help but think that my bike covered his protectively, like I always tried to do with him.

I paused and searched through my purse. I'd forgotten the lock. *Oh well, I just needed butter. It would only take a second.*

Anthony was still young enough to hold my hand in the store and maybe that's another big reason why I invited him to come on the holiday bike ride.

In the checkout line I thumbed through a home decorating magazine and looked with envy at the beautiful Christmas decorations that colored each page. How could I ever replace all those ruined decorations?

I felt a tug on my shirt and glanced down at my son.

"The lady wants your money," he said to me.

I looked up at the cashier and paid her a couple of bucks for the butter. For some reason the ten-dollar bill I'd received from the coupon felt too special to spend on butter.

I placed it in my purse, grabbed my son's hand, and walked outside. The bright sun pricked at my eyes and I squinted down at our bikes. Something was wrong. We walked closer.

Yes, something was definitely wrong.

The little bike, tucked protectively beneath mine, was gone.

The Christmas Bike

My bike looked lonely as it rested on the ground with handlebars twisted and seat scuffed.

A quick grab and go situation.

On Christmas Eve, in front of everyone, someone had stolen my son's bike.

Chapter Five

I'm not a violent person. I'm not even a competitive person. So when I say that I had dark thoughts come to mind about how I wanted to torture this thief, it might offer a small sample of my rage.

I wanted blood the color of holly berries.

I wanted to stuff their guts into Christmas stockings and poke their eyeballs out with candy canes.

I was a cookie stuffed teddy bear that turned into a momma grizzly, with my claws out, looking for revenge.

The image of how my bike had been leaning over his, shielding it from the threats of life, flashed to mind. My chest burned. I can't even sacrifice myself for my son's sake. Threats will always come.

When my shock waned, I glanced around the parking lot, which was bustling with people. Someone had seen this happen, yet no one had stopped it. What a crazy world we live in.

My boy wailed beside me when he finally realized that his bike was gone.

I spun around, hoping to see someone driving away or running away with proof of his or her crime. My hands went into fists to stop them from shaking in anger. I wanted to ring them around someone's neck.

What horrible thoughts to have on Christmas Eve.

Who steals a child's bike on the most giving holiday of the year?

No one stopped to ask why my son was bawling. People had groceries and rushing home on their minds.

An ache simmered in my chest. I wished for my angel friends, the ones that gave me baklava and the ten-dollar coupon. *They* would have stopped. Not that I expected anything, but *they* would have stopped at least to ask if I was okay and if my son was hurt.

And he was hurt . . . oh yes, he had been sliced through. The crazy world he had been born into had finally caught up with him and had been shattered as he tried to comprehend when I'd told him his bike had been stolen.

I'd choked the words out.

I thought to call my husband to pick us up, but not every problem is so easily solved. I had to fix this by myself. Besides, my bigger bike wouldn't fit in his little car anyway, and my piece of junk car was in the driveway with a dead battery or whatever its problem was.

We'd have to walk a longish way home. Would we make it in time for us to leave for the ice blocking tailgate party?

I cursed at the thief. What were they thinking? They'd left my boy without a ride and what took us fifteen minutes to bike would take us an hour to walk.

Who steals a child's bike at a grocery store, out in the open, leaving the poor child to walk home, with him knowing every little step, that his bike had been stolen?

On Christmas Eve.

Who does that?

I couldn't look at my boy's face any more. His large tears made my heart sink to my toes. My throat was burning. Hot tears were close, but the anger of it all kept them at bay. I enveloped my sweet boy in the biggest hug of his life. His small hands grasped around my neck.

"I'm so sorry, Anthony," I said in a raspy voice.

He held me tighter and I picked him up. I didn't care that I was making a scene. I cracked my eyes open at the people who passed me with a sobbing child in my arms. They'd glance at us and quickly look away. These people didn't care about other people, I decided. There is greed, and selfishness, and *theft*. There is no love of Christ. Santa replaced Him.

A man dressed up in a Santa costume rang his bell beside me. People threw a few coins in his bucket and hustled through the store doors.

Maybe it was easier to have a drive-by charity option. Coins in, charity out. No connection, no interaction. Just give a few coins and give yourself a guilt-free personal pat on the back.

I wasn't a charity case, true. I didn't want to be. But I needed someone—anyone—to ask if we were okay, because we most definitely were not. A huge part of my son's innocence had just been stolen. A large portion of my faith in humanity had been ripped from me. I'd been working retail for years, even before the bakery, so I'd seen the under belly of humanity, especially during Christmas. This was so much more.

I shook my head and buried it deep into my son's shoulder.

I thought of a few lines from my favorite Christmas song,

And in despair I bowed my head
There is no peace on earth I said
For hate is strong and mocks the song
Of peace on earth, good will to men.

I placed my boy's feet back on the ground and kicked up my kickstand. It was because of my own stupidity that it had been stolen. I was so stupid to think that nothing would happen during the ten minutes that we'd be inside the grocery store.

I was stupid to trust in people for ten minutes—a measly ten minutes.

Chapter Six

We crossed at the crosswalk, hand in hand. I'm sure my son looked wounded as he dragged his feet beneath him. When we'd reached the corner, we stopped and I wiped his face with the sleeve of my shirt. We walked a few more yards and then my son sat down on a patch of grass because he couldn't walk and sob at the same time. I lowered my bike to the ground and sat beside him.

I wrapped my arm around his shoulders and leaned my head on his blond curls. It would take a long time before we could afford to buy him another bike. My stomach twisted in knots, wishing that I could magically fix this.

My sisters would have had a bike they could've handed down to him. There were so many parts of my life they didn't know about anymore. Little details that we would have discussed over our Thai food lunch dates. Maybe I would have even laughed about this whole thing with them. They didn't know how bad we were hurting financially. They didn't know that I'd cried, longing for them, on many occasions driving on my long commute to and from work.

Memories were poison and the results made my heart hurt so badly that it felt like it would shrivel up and die.

I didn't notice someone had pulled a car over on the side of the road until that person stood before us. I looked up.

A handsome middle-aged man stood in a crisp pair of slacks and a clean white button up shirt with the sleeves rolled up to his elbows. I could smell his cologne.

"Are you two all right?" he asked. "Is he hurt?"

A caring person after all. I sighed.

I craned my neck to look behind him and saw a black convertible sports car with the top down. I looked up again at the worried look on his face. His thick brown hair was ruffled, probably from the convertible.

My gaze traveled down to his polished shoes. I shook my head. "Thanks for stopping, but we're fine."

I had wanted someone to stop at the grocery store and ask if we were okay. He was kind to stop and ask.

His silver watch shone in the sun and reminded me of all the shiny things I didn't have.

"My bike was stolen." My son blurted out.

I cringed and looked up at the man's eyes.

He paused. "Seriously? That's harsh." His voice implied a life of luxury and smooth sailing.

"We're okay, really," I said, pleading my case. *Were we okay?* Yes, we were going to be fine; this was just a small blow. *Nothing to see here,* I thought, feeling embarrassed and wishing the rich man would go away. *Thanks for stopping, but move along, please.*

I knew it had been kind of him to stop, so why did it bother me? Maybe it was because I couldn't relate to this guy at all. We were in different spheres. Our Christmases would probably be complete opposites.

"Sorry, little dude," he said. "You need to write an emergency letter to Santa, kid." He winked at me. "I'm sure you'll see a Christmas miracle."

My face paled as I looked at the man who had stopped to check on us, but who, in the end, had made things worse. So much worse.

Are you kidding me? I can't just up and go buy a bike. Even Santa can't pull that off.

"Thanks for stopping," I said between gritted teeth.

The man waved casually, turned for his sports car, and whipped away, leaving a trail of good intentions behind him.

Anthony looked up at me. His eyes were big with the realization that, upon writing a letter, Santa could simply touch his nose, twinkle his eyes, and inform the elves to place an emergency bike order.

Oh no. No, no, no.

His eyes were filled with so much hope and excitement that it cracked through and pierced my heart.

"I'm going to write a letter to Santa," he beamed. "I *know* he will bring me a new bike." He pulled on my arm. "Let's go!"

The tears had dried on Anthony's cheeks and he yanked me to standing. I held my son's hand while my other one wrapped around the handle of my bike. It was precarious and awkward to hold the bike while he pulled me anxiously forward. No one would stop us again and wonder if we were hurt. A kind gesture for him to stop, sure, but that wasn't exactly the kind of concern I wanted, or needed, from humanity just now.

I peeked down at my son. His face was splotchy but showed signs of hope and determination. He chatted about addressing the envelope and using express mail to get it to the North Pole quickly.

Maybe I could just say Santa never received the letter. I could totally do that. Ahh, but his face . . . his face held so much hope.

Cars whizzed past, hurrying home for Christmas Eve preparation. I wouldn't have time to make the dessert for tonight. I'd have to improvise with pudding or some quick fix. Ice cream. Did I have peppermint ice cream? I thought so and felt my shoulders relax beneath the backpack carrying only my sticks of butter, wallet, and child's bike helmet.

My son had a helmet, but no bike.

Anger ripped beneath my skin, making it feel hot.

There were a million things to do today, and fighting crowds and shopping sales for bikes were not on my list. Nor did I have the money.

But Anthony had faith that Santa Clause would bring him a bike.

Heaven help me, if we'd have to go into even more debt, Anthony would get his bike. Because that's what a good momma did and I promised myself that my house would be filled with love and laughter this Christmas, not tears.

Chapter Seven

After I explained the situation to my husband, we both decided that he would take the kids ice blocking while I would take his car and search in desperation for a bike from Santa.

Curse Santa. Why does he always get the credit anyway?

Brent arranged another family to pick them up for the ice blocking tradition that we'd hoped would fill in the holes of living away from family.

Determination to find a bike for my baby burned in my mind. After waving good-bye, I closed the door behind my family and cracked my knuckles.

I ran to my husband's car, spun it into reverse, and then pushed toward the stores. Two hours would be plenty of time to find a bike. I might even have time to make it to the dessert round of the tailgate party. Dessert, why were my thoughts always on dessert? You'd think by now I would have overdosed on them.

I huffed and puffed through the doors of the first store. No use. Nothing. All the children's bikes were gone. I sprinted back out and sped to the next store.

Maybe I did have a bit of competition inside of me. *I will find a bike!*

My aspirations were dashed a bit when two more stores came up short.

I dialed my husband's number. "I don't think I'll make it to any of the ice blocking."

"How is it out there, Santa?" he teased.

"Crazy! I'm glad to know that I'm not the only lazy, last minute parent," I said.

"You're not lazy or last minute," he said with an electric voice. He hated my self-loathing whenever I talked about what a lame mother I was. "Going out there proves it."

"Maybe so," I said. "I'm going to head over to Baseline and look for bikes."

"Be careful. There are a lot of desperate people out today."

I thought about the stolen bike. "Ya think?" I said sarcastically. "Thanks, babe. Love you."

I sped onto I-10 and the cars soon came to a stop. The traffic around Phoenix was enough to make anyone crazy and I really didn't feel like dealing with it on my day off from work. I had enough of it an hour each way, every day. Every single day.

I blasted up the Christmas carols and rolled down my windows. The person in the car next to me looked over and scowled at my attempt at holiday cheer. I gritted my teeth to keep my tongue in my mouth. *I'm trying over here.* I turned up the volume another notch, even though it was a really poppy Christmas song that I was sure would be stuck in my head all day.

I smiled sarcastically then looked forward.

Once off the freeway, at every stoplight, beggars were on the corners holding up cardboard signs. There always seemed to be more homeless people during the winter months and less when the heat rose above one hundred and ten for thirty days straight. Smart, but I wondered where they went when it turned into a scorching oven outside.

When at a red light, I glanced over to a man who stared into my window. I thought about not even having a penny in my purse when my balance was $50.01 at the grocery store. The ten-dollar bill from the coupon was still there, but I just couldn't give it to him, could I? It was that awkward moment when it looked like I was digging through my purse, as I debated. The man stepped forward.

The light turned green and saved me in my decision. I mean, I couldn't hold up traffic, so I stepped on the gas just as I saw the man's shoulders droop. I felt terrible. Really terrible. I wish I had loose change in my car, but I'd already gone through both cars days before, looking for change to buy slushies for the kids.

I told myself no more red lights. I'd speed through the yellows to avoid the beggars. How was I any better than the people who didn't stop as I held Anthony outside of the grocery store while he cried on my shoulder?

I groaned. I was a part of humanity; therefore I guess it was in my nature to not help others. Ugh, I wondered if my baklava friend and turquoise jewelry lady would have given the beggars money. Probably.

I pulled up to a large department store and ran inside.

"Nothing?" I asked after I'd searched the bike aisles. "How about in the back?"

"No." The employee looked at me with weary eyes. I knew that look. It was a look of working too much retail over the holidays. He lifted up a sarcastic smile. "We've been out of children's bikes for over a week. Most places are. Shoulda thought about getting a bike sooner than Christmas Eve."

My face felt boiling hot. My breath started coming out fast and heavy. I punched at my purse that hung limp and near empty at my side. I spun on my heel and sprinted out of the toy department without saying anything more to the guy.

Leaving the store, they were passing out free orange slices in the produce department. I took one, then walked out to the parking lot. Citrus fruits were the best in Arizona. I thought of our huge lemon tree in the yard and how I was planning on making lemonade for Christmas breakfast. Before living in the desert, I would have thought it cool if a neighbor gave me a bushel of lemons on Christmas with a cute saying like, "Turn your lemons into lemonade," or some cheesy thing like that. Here in Phoenix, it's more of a burden to receive extra lemons. I mean, there are only so many things to do with lemons.

Memories of homemade applesauce and canned peaches and apricot jam that I used to make when we lived in a cooler climate, came to mind. Mmm, and the apple crisps and raspberry pies and . . .

Climbing into my car, I tried to focus on the tart and tasty orange. But my thoughts always wandered back to a life that seemed as distant to me as a misty horizon. I dwelled too much on the past, but when there was no hope of blooming in a place where every plant wanted to kill you, I couldn't help but remember the good old times.

Memories are a funny thing. I wasn't plagued with coveting my neighbors or friends. Being a working mother made me feel guilty at times, but I didn't harbor jealousy for stay-at-home mothers, well mostly.

I was plagued by something deeper.

I was plagued by my own memories. I was insanely jealous of my past self. It made it hard to move on. My roots were somewhere else. Not in sandy, rocky soil.

My daughter, who I'd named after a tree, once said it perfectly, "Mom, I feel like I've been dug up and placed in a pot and moved to the desert."

I'd lied to her back then when I responded, "Oh girl, you will plant yourself here and have new experiences and make new friends and will soon love it."

I was such a little liar. I felt exactly like she did. My memories of once being planted in rich black soil were poisoning me.

I drove to three more department stores and all the employees said the same things, making me feel worse and worse. I tried pleading with some, as if they were elves and could magically make a bike appear.

I hated the concept of Santa. *That generous bugger who bestows gifts to greedy people.* It turned us—well, me—mad with desperation. Sure the concept of giving was all good and noble, but really, there was no joy in what I was doing. All of this running around with frantic abandon was because of a letter from a child and a promise of false hope from the big fat guy in a red suit.

Something told me that the repercussions of not producing a bike from Santa would be just as upsetting to my little boy as when it had been stolen in the first place.

Dear Santa,

You suck.

Chapter Eight

I headed my car homeward. The sun set early in Phoenix during the winter months and it was beginning to sink painfully close to the horizon, telling me that my efforts were in vain.

The Christmas-lit palm trees along the freeway started blinking to life in the dusty twilight. They stood tall, stretching into the amber sky like sawed off candy canes or straight lampposts at the North Pole. Even after living in Phoenix for a few seasons, it was hard to get used to living in a place where it didn't snow.

I looked to the west. Sunsets were my favorite aspect of living in the desert. Tonight it didn't disappoint as the sky turned to orange with streaks of crimson and purple glazing the low clouds.

I came up with a million ways to explain to Anthony why Santa hadn't brought a bike. The letter got lost in the mail. Santa was already delivering gifts to kids living on the opposite side of the world. Or maybe an elf stole the letter.

No. No elf *stealing* things, bad scenario.

My house would not be filled with love and laughter this Christmas.

I sped the car toward home and into the fading dusk. My heart ached as I watched the closed signs flicker to life early on the storefronts. I passed a high-end bike shop that I'd only gone into once when I'd been dreaming about a new bicycle for myself.

I swerved to the right lane and caused a few angry honks. One last stop. I waved as the tires spun into the parking lot and then turned off the car.

"Do you have any children's bikes?" I asked the employee when I'd gone inside and didn't see any on the floor.

The tall man grinned. "You're in luck. I just had a return an hour ago. Let me grab it." He walked around the checkout desk and came back with a gleaming blue bike. The perfect size and color!

I grasped my hands around the handlebars and pressed on the brakes. It would be perfect, but something told me it wouldn't be the cheap discount store bike that I'd been shopping for all day.

"How much?" I hated being so blunt, but I'd had enough and I just wanted to be home.

"On sale for two hundred thirty."

I gulped and felt my cheeks burn. I couldn't even entertain purchasing a bike for that much . . . could I? I thought of my credit cards and knew they were all maxed out. I'd be charged an overdraft fee. So, two hundred thirty, plus a thirty-five dollar overdraft fee. I rang my hands together. I hadn't eaten any lunch, but I still felt nauseated.

How much was a smile on my child's face worth?

Was it worth it for Santa to go into debt and beyond?

The Christmas Bike

I took so long that the clerk left me and began to start closing shop. My fingers caressed the bike seat then the frame. As a family, we did go on bike rides a lot. It was free entertainment and a release for Brent and I after work. What would we do if Anthony didn't have a bike and couldn't come with us because of it?

I wiped my hand over my face and tried to make a firm decision. That was a car payment, or grocery money, or payment for my kids to be on sports teams. All of which were lacking.

"I can't." I heard myself say. I didn't even realize I'd said it out loud. Must have been my subconscious telling me how ridiculous it would be to spend that kind of money right now.

The clerk shrugged. "I can probably go two hundred even. Only because it's Christmas Eve."

A punch to the gut.

The truth that I still couldn't afford it hurt.

"I'm sorry," I said, hustling for the door before I changed my mind and he could see my face. "Merry Christmas."

Inside the car I sat limp and deflated.

So, that was it. Anthony would have a horrible Christmas.

I leaned my head against the headrest and felt a great and terrible headache emerge from the depths of frustration.

It was just me in the car, but sitting in the passenger's side were my inadequacies. My failures. My doubts. Incurable feelings that plagued me.

I listened to the silence, not wanting to go home just yet.

My phone rang. Brent. I clicked it off.

I watched the clerk through the storefront's "frosty" windows hang the perfect little bike on a hook and then go to the back and turn off a light.

I guess I should go home, I thought. I clicked over the key in my husband's car and nothing happened. A pit dug into my stomach. *No, no. Not this car too. Please.* I flipped it over again, pressed on the gas, but it was completely dead. I threw the keys onto the passenger seat and swore.

I breathed for a long time. In and out. In and out. Because, at this point, what else was there to do? I closed my eyes and felt utterly alone. I'd been taught to pray and had believed in miracles at different times in my life. Was I worthy to receive one? Nope.

Well, maybe it was worth a shot.

"Please, God," I whispered in my car. "I know I haven't talked to you much these days, or months, or has it been years? I've just been busy, you know." A large lump began to rise up my chest and into my throat. It burned me on the inside.

"I just feel . . . abandoned."

Whoa, where did that come from? The dam had burst. I gulped for air as tears flowed down my cheeks.

Abandoned.

"You misled me." Words and tears flowed out of me. "I thought I followed so many intuitions from you. But they ended up leading me, us, down gut-wrenching paths. Is that really what you wanted me to experience? Did you really want me to end up like this? In a place where I am merely surviving and not thriving? Am I destined to live a monotonous life, full of good intentions, but too busy and broken to do anything about them? Am I destined to give out broken cookies to others in place of my own talents?" I spoke louder. "I really don't think sugar fixes everything." I grasped the steering wheel and shook it.

What a one-sided conversation.

Maybe that's why I hadn't prayed much to my Father these days.

"The hurts seem to keep on resurrecting themselves." I spoke aloud. "I'll think I've forgiven others, but then something else, more painful, happens. I'll think that forgiveness has been granted to me, but then I'll see selfishness and hate in other people and wonder if I'll ever be forgiven."

My body trembled.

"WHY?" I yelled.

Silence.

"For what? What was all of it for?"

Silence.

The silence and emptiness settled beneath my skin. Buried down into the deepest, most abandoned parts of myself.

I took a deep breath, wiped my tears, and closed my eyes. *You know what? I'm glad the car broke down. I can't face my family anymore. They can have Christmas without me. I can't watch Anthony's face when he realizes that Santa is a sham. That his mom is a sham. That life is a sham.*

Silence was the only response.

Too much silence.

A tap on my window broke through the silence and made me jump in the seat.

I looked up and saw the clerk through the muted glass. How had I cried so much that the windows of the car were fogged up? I leaned into the door and rolled down the window.

"Need a jump?"

I gulped down the last of my tears.

Did I really want to stay in this car overnight and miss Christmas?

"I think so," I said to him.

Was it "*I think so*" that I wanted to sleep in the car and miss Christmas? Or was it "*I think so*" that I needed a jump so I could go home to my family?

That was the million-dollar question.

I waited so long that he asked me again.

"Yes, yes I need help. I want to go home to my family," I finally said.

"I'm just locking up, then I'll grab my jumper cables."

"Thanks."

I lifted up a corner of my lips and attempted to smile in his direction. As he walked away I rested my forehead on the steering wheel. I slumped, listening to my breathing and the silence that wasn't so much silence anymore.

Something told me to look up and across the street.

Chapter Nine

A church—I didn't even know which denomination—had an impressive Nativity set up on a front lawn. I glanced at Mother Mary and then down to the Christ Child. Then back up to Mary. She had a face full of peace and contentment. A face full of the love of a mother for her son. A face I really wanted to emulate to my own children.

My gaze dropped to the bundle lying in the manger. Had I thought of Christ *once* this entire frantic holiday season?

No, I believe I had not.

I stared at the Christ Child. He had been born into humble means.

He didn't care about things. He cared about people.

The gifts He gave were never *things*.

Love and laughter were filled through people, not things, I realized.

As those words sank into my heart, I understood that Christ's love for us was beyond measure. God's love for me, personally, as his daughter, would never be shown through *things*. It would be shown by the Spirit and by the incredible people who shared my life.

My gaze skimmed over to the sculptures of angels in the Nativity.

So many angels had come into my life over the past twenty-four hours. My heart softened as I stared at their beautifully sculpted mouths, singing praises to their King.

I listened to the silence in my car. Embraced it. Became a part of the silence, and I began to realize that it wasn't silence.

It never had been.

God had always answered my prayers.

He had never abandoned me.

Never.

He had placed angelic people into my life over the past few days, and months, and years to fill in the silence for him and to make me not feel abandoned. Yet me, and my chatty, disbarring thoughts, made it impossible to notice that all of those people came from Him.

My chest began to burn hot. It swelled with an intense love that I hadn't felt for such a long time. I was starved for it. My heartbeat began to race with renewed hope and a smile pulled on my cheeks. So much love flooded into me.

Suddenly, it really didn't matter at all if I magically produced a bicycle.

I thought of the thief and felt an incredible amount of sympathy for that person, whoever they were. They probably had fewer things than I had and they probably felt more abandoned than I did.

Who was I to let someone else's actions determine who I'd let myself become?

The Christmas Bike

The bike shop clerk tapped on my window and I grinned up at him. He seemed a bit shocked at my newfound genuine smile.

I popped the hood, and in no time, my husband's car sputtered back to life.

"Thank you so much!" I said with gusto and a large smile. "Merry Christmas!"

"Merry Christmas to you too."

I reversed and turned onto the main street toward home. I wanted to share the Christmas spirit with my children and husband. It seemed to be running through my veins and I couldn't drive fast enough.

I passed a store with a blinking open sign still in the window. A thought burst to my mind and I peeled over to the side and pulled into the parking lot that was almost empty. Just one last store.

Why hadn't I thought of the local thrift shop before?

I didn't want to turn the car off, for fear that the battery would die, and so I rolled down the passengers window an inch and then locked the doors as the car was running. I could shove a stick easily in there and unlock the door. If there were more thieves out there who needed a car, so be it. My heart was bursting with too much love for people to think otherwise.

The store was closing in exactly seven minutes. More than enough time to quickly take a peek. The night was beginning to settle around me, turning into what promised to be a magical Christmas Eve. I'd spent the entire afternoon frazzled, when I should have been with my family.

A little prayer played on my lips. It felt foreign and yet so familiar to pray for even the small things. "Please. Please.

I'm just running in. Let there be a little bike. Let my car be safe. Please."

I raced through the doors and sprinted to the back.

Behind a large fake Ficus plant, I saw the hint of a little tire and I stopped.

My hands went to my stomach. *Please be a bike.*

I walked closer and froze.

There it sat, waiting patiently for me the whole day. Over the course of the day, it had waited for me to silence my mind enough to be able to really listen.

I'm not going to admit that I ugly cried in the thrift store. That would just be weird. But it might have happened.

Okay, it did happen.

I bawled.

Only because I was filled with so much gratitude. I'd just gone on a wild goose chase, or should I say bike chase.

Only to circle around back home.

The store was only a few miles from my neighborhood. If I had stopped there first, I would have grabbed the bike, shoved it in my trunk, and gone about the rest of the day, not knowing about the struggle it took me to get here.

I wouldn't have prayed.

I wouldn't have thought about Christ.

I wouldn't have found sympathy for the thief.

I took a few steps closer. This bike was in better condition than the one that was stolen; Anthony's stolen bike had been a hand-me-down, first given from a cousin to my middle son, and then handed down to Anthony.

I only saw a few scratches on the bicycle's paint, which could easily be covered up by a red paint pen that I knew I had at home in my art supplies. Anthony would never notice anything was ever wrong.

I grasped my hands around the rubber handle bar grips and wheeled it to the front. Even both tires were full of air!

I leaned my face down into my shoulder and swiped at my tears before I got to the cashier who looked tired.

"I can't believe I found this bike!" I exclaimed. "I've searched everywhere."

"That's cool," she said while snapping her bubble gum. "That'll be $9.95."

I pulled out the crisp ten-dollar bill that had been given to me because of the coupon I received from the jewelry lady at the grocery store.

I beamed with pride. What a circle!

It blew my mind how connected all the angels in my life had been today and yesterday.

The fifty-dollar bill from the baklava person made it so that I could go to the grocery store. Then, I received the coupon that gave me ten dollars back so that I would have the money and not go into debt by paying for this perfect little bike with cash.

"Merry Christmas!" I said in a hearty voice. I headed for the door, since I was anxious that the piece of junk car was still idling in the parking lot.

"Hey, do you want your five pennies?" the employee asked.

I thought of how embarrassing it had been for me earlier to dig around and not even have an extra penny to my name. My foot pushed the kickstand down and I walked back to her.

"Yes. Yes, I do want those pennies."

She looked at me weird.

"Every bit helps," I said, shrugging my shoulders with feigned indifference.

Who knew where these pennies were going to end up. I placed them in the zipper coin pocket in my purse and pushed the bike out the door. Maybe I'd always keep them as a last reminder of the fifty-dollar bill.

Those five pennies were still part of the circle.

Chapter Ten

I sat watching the smiles of my children on Christmas morning.

There was probably another child who was smiling this morning too. Even if the guilt ate at the parent who had stolen the bike, the child would never know where it had come from and was happy.

I nestled my head onto the capable chest of Brent and looked at our only decoration that survived the melted wax and rat fiasco. The hand-carved Nativity from Jerusalem sat on our mantle and stood as a reminder to our family to remember Christ during Christmas. The sculpted olive wood looked shiny and new after a good wash. As all of our decorations had been destroyed, the only one that really mattered was the Nativity.

Like the Nativity at the church, where I had finally prayed, it would forever remind me of the true meaning of Christmas.

I closed my eyes and played out several scenarios of who stole the bike:

A single mother, who works three jobs to put food on the table, saw a bike that could fit her son. As she stuffed her few dollars in her ratty purse and walked into the grocery store, she thought of a way to get the bike. She has barely enough money to pay for a gallon of milk that she will make into a chocolate pudding for Christmas dessert. Her son will have no Christmas at all. The bike could help him with his balance and social skills and because they could never afford sports, it would also be a way for him to exercise. A bike would give him happiness and a taste of self-confidence.

Or maybe the thief was a teenage boy who'd stolen the bike for his little brother who gets bullied every day at school. And because he only got a few hours at work a week during Christmas, he didn't have enough money to get anything for his younger brother. His deadbeat parents maybe didn't even remember that it was Christmas. The bike would give them something to do together. They could bike away from their home life together whenever it got too intense. He'd grabbed the bike in front of all the shoppers, but his drive to put a smile on his younger brother's face fueled his motivation. And he was a fast sprinter. He'd had plenty of practice sprinting away from his abusive father.

Or maybe, simply put, a poor father had three children who would all fit the bike. Maybe it was a family gift from Santa. Maybe the father justified his actions by thinking that it would put smiles on three children's faces, and not just one.

If someone was desperate enough to steal a child's bike on Christmas Eve, they had bigger problems than I did.

I opened my eyes when my favorite Christmas carol, "I Heard the Bells on Christmas Day," played over the radio and listened quietly to the last verse of the song.

Then pealed the bells more loud and deep

The Christmas Bike

God is not dead, nor doth he sleep
The wrong shall fail, the right prevail,
With peace on earth, good will to men.

Did it matter who had stolen the bike? Did the scenario matter? Whoever had done this had a great enough motivation to potentially ruin a child's Christmas Eve.

I forgave the person, whoever they were.

It was actually pretty easy to do.

Peace fell upon me like a warm blanket. My husband must have felt it too, because he squeezed me into him further. My kids were laughing, unbroken cookies were baking, and a deep sense of love flooded into me.

Christmas had brought *things*, but we also had a home full of Christ and I made a commitment to carry more of Him throughout the new year.

Maybe my roots were beginning to take root. Did it matter where I lived? As long as I was with my family and we focused on having a Christ-centered home, did it matter if the soil was rocky and sandy? No, it didn't. Roots adapt and spread, but only when they are fed. I promised myself that I'd stop moaning, especially internally, about our situation. I'd focus on making my roots strong. With strong roots, I could bloom wherever I was planted.

After the presents were unwrapped and the green-and red-colored pancakes eaten, I asked Anthony what his very favorite gift was that he received.

"Christmas is for *giving* gifts, Mom. Don't you know?"

Maybe I had done something right. Maybe I had taught them something good.

I smiled and looked into my children's eager faces and said, "Christmas is also for forgiving people. That is the greatest gift of all."

Christmas is for giving gifts.
Christmas is for forgiving people.

Chapter Eleven

Dear Anthony,

Thank you for writing your last-minute letter. I received it just in time.

There are many people who make my naughty list every year. I'm sorry you were a victim to one of them. But, among the seemingly endless bad, there is also much good. I hope you will always be a warrior and an example of truth and righteousness. Do this and your life will always be blessed.

Love,
Santa

P.S. Thank you for being a good little boy this year.

Epilogue

This story is true. Much too true, I'm afraid.

Every Christmas since, I've wondered where that bike went. The mystery shall remain a mystery and maybe those are the best kind. I realize it probably won't be as glamorous as I've purported in my head. I'd like to think that it went to a little child who didn't receive enough love and came from meager means.

I like to think about the thief. When they placed my son's bike beneath their own Christmas tree, were they ashamed? Did they have guilt when they looked into their smiling child's face? Did they think about my own child and the tears that followed? What drove them to steal?

I think about the woman with the turquoise jewelry who'd given me a ruffled up coupon that made it possible, in the end, to purchase a bike. Was it her generous personality to always think of others? In my mind, I imagine her spreading kindness and listening to her inner charitable voice and noticing the needs of others. I try to follow her example and do little tiny things for others. I mean, it was a *coupon*. Something so insignificant. So, if something so small has still stuck with me all these years, how much would something large affect someone? People remember small acts of kindness. I have tried to implement this in my own life.

Epilogue

I also think about my friend or neighbor who lovingly made my family a pan of homemade baklava with a card attached, containing a fifty-dollar bill. I know this person was a fellow baker. I mean, I've baked professionally for years and have never attempted baklava. In truth, this person made this entire story possible. Their act of kindness snowballed me to be able to go to the grocery store and buy food and new Christmas tree ornaments. Which in turn, allowed me to spend exactly fifty dollars that made it possible to use the coupon the woman gave me. Which then left me with exactly the right amount of money to purchase a secondhand bike. I've narrowed it down to four people who I think it could've been. I will send each of them a copy of this book. If you still wish to remain anonymous, just know what your kindness meant to me. I thank you with all of my heart.

Mostly I like to think about my former self back then. Not with sadness, heaven's no, but with smiles. Those lean years shaped me. It made me compassionate toward the mind of a helpless thief. There were times that I entertained what sins I would commit to give my kids an abundant Christmas. My morals just never let me dip so low. But I understand the deep, consuming despair of not giving your children all that you think they deserve. The lean years tenderized me to people who are in need, especially during Christmas. I can say, without a doubt, that I had bloomed where I'd been planted in Phoenix. Looking back, I thought that my roots were withering and that the pressure and heat of our lean experiences were killing me. Now, I see just how much they had shaped me. And I'd made some pretty incredible friends, obviously, because . . . baklava.

Epilogue

I've always written poetry and I've always written my thoughts down, but Phoenix is where I turned those ramblings into novels. Writing novels was my way of escaping my scorching reality. What better way to find your true passion than through the fiery temperament of soul searching and pain?

My family and I have moved back to a place where it snows during Christmas. Geographically I'm happier, but I've come to realize that you can bloom wherever you are planted, *especially* in the desert. You can see the beauty of the summer monsoons, or the incredible sunsets, or the blooming saguaro cactus just as much as the beauty of majestic mountains, aspen trees, and four seasons. There is beauty everywhere and in everyone, you just have to look for the hidden gems.

Because of this true experience, I have made it a point to give bikes to children in need. Children deserve to have their letters to Santa granted and their prayers to Christ answered.

Acknowledgments

A big thank you, first and foremost, to my husband, Matt, for your eternal love and support. To my children, who I know think their mom is crazy. I love catching you talking about my books and ideas to your friends. You make me a proud parent. To my mom and dad, who love me unconditionally and encourage me in my endeavors. To my siblings and my in-laws, I couldn't wish to be part of a better family. To my friends and fellow tribe, you inspire me to see the world differently.

To my sisters, Tonya, Tamra, and Traci. I wrote this book as a Christmas gift to you. I appreciate your love and encouragement to publish this book. I am so grateful that we live closer again so we can have our Thai food lunch dates. You are my best friends!

A special shout-out goes to my Anwa Storyteller sistas and critique buds: Laura, Nicole, Christine W., Jodi, Susan, Jenelle, Diana, Kristy, Stacy, Barbara, Jen W., Christine S., Emily, and Angie. You were the first and only people outside of my family to see this book. Your talent amazes me and I am constantly lifted and enriched by each of you. Also to

Acknowledgments

my Night Sprint buds: Alice, Crystal, Lauri, Jen, Courtney, Kate, Michael, and Emily. Thank you for burning the midnight oil with me. I wrote this entire book during all those late nights.

To Jenny and Michelle, you lived through this with me, thank you. Jenny, brainstorming books with you was my favorite part of Phoenix.

To the team at Cedar Fort, Inc.: editors, proofreaders, designers, and marketers. Thank you for working with me and believing in this story.

Most of all, I am grateful for my desire and obsession to create things. I know that comes from a higher power, and I thank God for his constant love for me.

About the Author

Tara Mayoros teaches guitar, paints, occasionally still bakes, and loves working with plants. She's an avid collector of globes and maps, since they help with her incurable case of wanderlust. The Rocky Mountains are her home, and they call to her whenever she is in need of inspiration. She explores them regularly with her husband and three children.

She is excited to announce that *The Christmas Bike* was given an award through the League of Utah Writers winter competition.

Tara's debut novel, *Broken Smiles* (Astraea Press/Clean Reads, 2014), was a finalist for the MBUN competition and a nominee for a Whitney Award. Her second novel, *Eight Birds for Christmas*, was also released in the same year. In the past, she has served as president of SL Storytellers and vice president of Phoenix Nightscrawlers. Tara is currently on the board of directors for LDStorymakers. One of her favorite aspects of being a published author is giving back to the stellar writing community and also all of the friendships she has made. To read more about Tara you can visit her online at taramayoros.com.